Fae Lights

SAMHAIN SHIFTERS SHORTS

AIMEE EASTERLING

Contents

Author's Note

The stories in this collection are a bit of a hodgepodge with two central themes—fae and happy endings. Some have characters that overlap with novels in the Samhain Shifters series, and a couple are so deeply embedded that I've labeled them with spoiler alerts. I hope all leave you with a smile on your face and extra magic in your day.

Briar Moon

Chapter 1

The first thing Frances noticed were the thorns. Long and sharp and the least of the dangers her father had warned against if she didn't wait for a private carriage to carry her back from California.

The second thing she noticed was the smile of the man in charge of the thorns. Frances's pulse quickened as his intense blue gaze caught hers, an instant awareness chasing away the dreariness that had dogged her footsteps ever since she left her father's hotel.

Fascination and danger warred within her. The man on the stage-coach seat across from her was a stranger, one of two actually. The pair cradled the thorny, leafless shrub between them while emanating a sense of physical vitality and latent power that reminded her of wolves at rest yet ready to spring.

Frances clutched her reticule tighter, remembering her father's warning about how rough the effluvia from Gold Rush towns could be. *"The mud in the street is nothing compared to the filth of the un-washed masses striding through it,"* he'd muttered, even such harsh words music on his lips.

He hadn't been harsh with Frances, of course. He'd kept her safe, clad in the very best day dresses and evening gowns. Perhaps a little too safe. Because she'd been perennially curious, craning her neck to see what her father so roundly criticized, wishing she didn't always have to stay cloistered and pristine.

She was curious now too. Pinched within her maid's ill-fitting dress, she had none of her father's wealth and prestige to protect her. Also none of his commands to keep her apart from the outside world.

So she met the smiling man's eyes rather than turning away as she ought to have. After all, how many times had her father warned that most men who came to California seeking gold ended up drifting back with dreams squashed and pockets empty? They were dangerous in the way of a stray dog too hungry to be trusted eating out of your hand.

But this man's eyes weren't tired. Instead, wild blue irises considered Frances so intently she was the one who looked away, out the wooden-slatted window at the craggy mountain landscape rushing past. It wouldn't be long now until the next stop. An opportunity to get off, to wait for another stagecoach...

To lose her nerve. Give up on adventure and return home to the safety of her father. Frances forced her body back erect. No, she wouldn't do that.

"Ever see gold nuggets straight out of the ground?" The man's voice was a low rumble, the exact same pitch as the metal wheels rolling across the ground beneath them. His words were quiet enough so Frances could have pretended not to hear him. Instead, she nodded. Some men had found gold; of course they had. And they'd spent good portions of it in her father's stores, where she had indeed enjoyed many opportunities to handle gold nuggets straight out of the ground.

The smiling man spoke again, as if her nod had been an invitation to continue the conversation. "This blackberry bush is ten times as precious."

Surprised, Frances met those wild blue eyes a second time. They twinkled. Drew her in closer until their knees touched.

Awareness turned into something considerably more powerful. Boulders blurred past in her peripheral vision and Frances struggled to catch her breath.

She should have listened to her father. Should have stayed within the gilded cage he'd created for her. She should have...

"Hey." The man pressed both of his long legs up against those of his sleeping companion, breaking their connection. And abruptly Frances could breathe again.

Only once she'd settled did the man retrieve a small knife from a sheathe at his belt and carefully whittle a six-inch sprig from one of the bush's branches. "Here."

He held out the twig and Frances had no reason to take it. Thorns waited to snag her and she had the strangest memory of lying in her bed two decades ago listening to a nursemaid spin a fairy tale about blood on a thorn. Blood and danger....

The next day, that nursemaid had been gone. Her father had tucked Frances into bed for a solid week after that until a new staff member was hired. The replacement pursed her lips and shook her head at any request for a story or song.

Now, despite her inability to recall much of the fragmented memory, Frances heeded its warning. Thorns weren't safe. For her especially.

But the man continued holding out the twig. And her curiosity demanded knowledge of what kind of bush could be more valuable than gold.

So she ignored the warning tremor inside herself and took the twig. Accepting it carefully between thumb and forefinger, the thorns turned out to be easy to avoid.

And she was glad she hadn't merely viewed the twig from a distance because it wasn't cool and dormant the way its leafless state suggested. Instead, the stem twirled warm between her fingers and when it stilled, she blinked.

How could she have missed the flower bud as large as her littlest fingernail at the tip?

"Ah," the man said. The stagecoach was slowing. Were they already at the next stop?

Frances was still trying to regain her composure when the smiler nudged his sleeping seat mate. For the first time, Frances took a real look at the other man, noting that he and the smiler shared perfectly carved features kissed by exactly the same amount of sun. Were they brothers?

If so, their similarities were only skin deep. Because the sleeper's blue eyes were far less interesting than the smiler's, and less interested also. His attention slid over Frances as if she was part of the landscape. Then he turned to the smiler and they hefted the blackberry bush between them.

The one with the wide smile tipped his hat at her. "A pleasure to meet you, ma'am." He thrust open the door and the pair disembarked.

Other than the fleeting moment when she'd considered running from the smiling stranger, Frances had no intention of getting off at this hole-in-the-wall town. The hamper at her feet was packed with cold meats, breads, cheeses, precious chocolate, and even coffee brewed fresh for her that morning. She had everything she needed to stay on the stagecoach until she reached one of her father's hotels several stops later. Doing so was safer and would be more comfortable as well.

But the flower bud on the twig swelled as she watched it. One petal curled itself open, then another.

Frances watched, fascinated. The flower's bloom made no sense, not in late October, not so quickly.

What also made no sense was her inability to stop thinking about the man with the over-wide smile.

The wheels beneath the stagecoach were already starting to turn when she shot to her feet and pushed the door open. Her button-trimmed ankle boots squished in the mud as she leapt out, calling up to the driver. "My valise!"

While she waited for the stagecoach driver to unload her luggage, Frances considered the town in which she found herself. Bleached wooden buildings lined either side of Main Street, lacking even a coat of paint to brighten hard edges. Worn dirt paths branched off haphazardly and only a red-lit saloon and the tiny hotel showed any signs of life.

The desolate town seemed an unlikely spot for adventures. But the smiling man *was* an adventure. Once Frances found him, she could ask...

What? Why this blackberry twig was blooming so far out of season? Why she couldn't get his smile out of her head?

Shaking away her confusion, Frances brushed dirt off the hem of a gown that, now, was less of an asset than it had been that morning.

The stagecoach driver tried to drop her valise in the mud, requiring the sight of coinage before he agreed to carry it to the hotel. And, once there, Frances was forced to request assistance by ringing a bell.

"A room?" the girl behind the counter asked, turning around to face her after far longer than Frances had ever been kept waiting.

"Yes," Frances answered, keeping her voice even although she knew her father would have snapped an angry set down in the face of such intentional slowness. "But first, would you be so kind as to direct me to my friends? They've checked in already. Two men carrying a blackberry bush between them..."

"Your *friends* walked right past our door and headed that way."

The girl was younger than Frances, but cheerfully competent and quite willing to call her bluff. Still, she did offer a pointed direction. South where the mountain loomed above their tiny town, causing evening to fall earlier than it would have in the flatlands.

The men with the blackberry bush had walked out of town into the darkness? Curiouser and curiouser, as the aspiring novelist Lewis Carroll liked to write in his correspondence with Frances's father.

"Please bring my luggage to my room," Frances requested, paying more than she needed to as her father had taught her. Overpayment won loyalty. Overpayment halted questions.

Then, rather than going after her valise, she strode out into the darkness, following the thin thread of a trail south.

Ever since Frances was a child, her night vision had been better than average. So she didn't stumble as mud gave way to stony ground and the already narrow trail turned even narrower. Her footing remained firm while the sun sank the rest of the way behind the mountain and night chill prickled the bare skin of her cheeks and neck.

She did, however, second guess the entire expedition when her legs began to burn with unaccustomed effort. What was she doing disobeying her father then thoughtlessly trailing strangers into the wilderness? At night. Without so much as a coat or a change of undergarments!

The twig twirled between her fingers as she pondered. And the flower continued to open until all five petals glowed like a star in the dark.

There'd been another story that nursemaid told her, hadn't there? Something about thorny hedges protecting a princess…

The memory was as hard to make out as the night-clouded horizon. Frances was still struggling to piece it all together when she rounded a bend and found an enormous wolf bristling in the middle of the path.

Chapter 2

In fur, it was easy for Duke to ignore his suspicions from the stagecoach. Yes, even when starlight glinted off the flower in the beauty's hand, the flower that shouldn't have been able to open so quickly on a twig whittled off a dormant blackberry bush, albeit a potentially magical one.

He took a step toward her, drawn by something he couldn't explain and didn't need to. There were flecks of gold in her wide, hazel eyes and her hair was as lustrous as a grackle's feathers. Meanwhile, her boots were far finer than her dress and handbag, a smart place to splurge if she was as poor as she appeared.

Somehow, though, Duke suspected there was more to her story. Especially since her cultured voice had boasted the crisp diction of the upper class.

He only realized he'd come so close she could have reached out and touched him when she did the exact opposite. Flinching away, her heart pounded so hard it tickled his eardrums, and Duke found himself lowering his belly to the earth by way of apology.

Suspicions or no suspicions, there was no cause to frighten a woman walking alone in the dark.

Even frightened, however, she didn't flee. Instead, she spoke in a way he suspected was meant to boost her own confidence. "Excuse me, wolf. I'm afraid you're in my way and I'll sprain my ankle if I leave the trail. Perhaps if I stay to one side you won't bite me as I pass..."

Suiting actions to words and tucking her skirts the same way she'd done while entering the stagecoach, she sidled closer to the drop-off that formed one edge of the path. Duke hadn't thought through his belly flop or he would have flopped in that direction to protect her from the cliff-side danger. Now, even quality boots weren't sufficient to save her from the crumble of loose earth beneath one foot and the loss of balance that came after.

"Oh!" she exclaimed, arms windmilling as she tipped toward the thirty-foot drop that led to jagged rocks and likely death.

He grabbed her. Shifted first, of course, even though a lady—and this woman was clearly a lady—would be mortified by a naked man coming at her out of the darkness.

He wasn't, however, about to let her fall.

Her waist was firm in his grip, her breath sweet when she panted out words that never quite formed sentences. "Who? What? I... How?"

It felt wrong, but Duke took advantage of her flustered state. When dealing with the fae, it was imperative to strike ironclad bargains and maintain the upper hand at all costs. So even though it tasted as if he'd tossed a handful of blackberries into his mouth then bitten down on a surprise stinkbug, he murmured, "A question from me for every question from you. Agreed?"

"Um. Yes?"

As she spoke, her flower-carrying hand settled onto his shoulder, light as a songbird coming to rest on a limb it thought might not hold its weight. He could hold her weight easily, of course. Could have carried her away from the drop-off and set her down on those expensive, practical boots in a spot where she had no chance of falling over any other ledges.

But she hadn't asked to be released and he was enjoying the press of her curves against his angles. Still, that stink-bug taste demanded he exhibit at least a modicum of the gentlemanly behavior his aunt had bitten into his ruff while he was a pup. "Ladies first. Ask me a question."

"Who are you?" She tilted her head to peer up at him and it was hard not to let his lupine side seize her interest and lean into it. To tell her everything about himself. To beg for her attention to stay riveted only on him.

Instead, he offered precisely what she'd asked for—his name. "Duke."

"You're a duke?"

He shook his head. "It's a family name, one in every generation. I'm Duke. My brother is Cyrus."

And there he was, running on at the mouth just like one might expect when faced with a fae who wanted answers. Duke clenched his jaw, ignored his inner wolf, and demanded: "That was two answers so I'm owed two also."

He expected her to argue, but the beauty only shrugged, the motion pulling fabric taut beneath the hand he still kept at her waist to steady her. Knowing he was owed two questions, he started with the same simple opening she had. "Who are you?"

"Frances. Not a family name. Just mine."

Her smile felt like butterfly iridescence caught in sunlight. Like heady wine swallowed in front of a warm fire with his pack all around him. Like the promise of something he'd spent his entire life knowing wasn't a dream he could grasp.

Duke clenched his jaw. Fae were glorious to look at and rotten at the center. He needed to stay smart for the sake of his brother and his pack.

Forcing his voice hard, he demanded, "Why were you following us?"

"Why?" She still clung to that twig with its unlikely flower and now she peered down as if the minuscule plant held all the answers. "I suppose I was curious. About this flower, although that was nothing compared to..."

Her words cut off as she motioned at his body, human now but lupine moments earlier. And he noted the moment she took in his complete nakedness. Her cheeks reddened and her breath caught. "Oh dear. I'm afraid I must ask you to don proper attire."

Not to put her down? Duke laughed, expecting her to flinch the way she had at the sight of the wolf's interest behind his human eyes back in the stagecoach. Instead, after the slightest of hesitations, she opened those blackberry-plump lips...and she laughed too.

Her chuckle was like a summer breeze cutting through overwhelming humidity. Like a ray of sunlight on a gray winter morning. Like warm molasses drizzled across a halved biscuit hot out of the oven.

She was fae. The way her laughter stroked his wolf's fur proved it.

So why did Duke succumb to the temptation his family taught him to avoid at all costs? Why did he lead her straight to the repurposed prospector's shack and invite her in?

Chapter 3

Frances peered into the dim space, smaller than her second-best shoe closet and with absolutely none of its amenities. The shack was lit by a kerosene lamp, which meant the cracks in the rough plank walls were a boon for letting out the foul-scented smoke. Other than a table and chair, the only nod to habitation was a pile of blankets on one side of the floor from which she caught the scritch of a mouse.

Which meant those tiny black pellets scattered across every surface were likely vermin excrement. Father would have expected her to succumb to vapors.

Instead, Frances kept her focus on the only dangerous part of her surroundings—Cyrus.

Duke's brother glared at her with eyes just as blue as the ones she'd peered into on the train but with something dark and feral lurking deep within his pupils. He opened his mouth, then shut it again. Grabbing his brother's shoulder, he knocked Frances aside while manhandling Duke out into the dark.

"What do you think you're doing?" The harsh whisper was far enough away so Frances shouldn't have been able to hear it. But her ears were as good as her eyes and she caught Cyrus's every word. "Do you think we have time for dalliance? Does Louisa mean nothing to you?"

Frances kept her back to the men, pretending to survey the space she'd already observed in its entirety. Meanwhile, questions tumbled through her head like unruly kittens.

Who was Louisa? Was Duke prone to bringing home strange women?

Duke's reply, when it finally came, answered neither of those questions. "Aunt Ellen always said to keep your friends close and your enemies closer."

Despite the fact that Frances had to be who he was referring to as an enemy, his words seemed to stroke up one side of her face and down the other. She shivered, wrapping her arms around her middle. The thorns on the blackberry twig snagged the fabric of her dress.

"So you brought her here?" This was Cyrus. His temper seemed to be cooling and he almost sounded like a gentleman when he added. "How do you intend to keep her from freezing tonight?"

"Allow that to be my problem. No sign of James?"

"None. But there was a letter. From—" Cyrus's voice lowered "—from Louisa."

Frances did turn then, just enough to catch sight of two dark shadows coming together outside the cabin. The brothers were the same height and it was impossible to distinguish them at a distance in the near pitch darkness. All she could tell was that one had leaned his head down to press against the other's shoulder. Brotherly arms pulled the mourner in close and Frances caught the faint gasp of a sob.

The excellent sandwich Frances had eaten for her dinner suddenly rebelled against further digestion, likely a cue that this intimate moment was not meant to be observed by a stranger. So she stepped further into the mouse-infested shack and turned her attention away from what was none of her concern.

She didn't intend to go hunting for the letter—also very clearly none of her concern. But it was sitting there on the table beside the kerosene lamp and her eyes picked out words before she could avert them. *Duke* and *our baby*. Despite the cold, Frances's cheeks flamed unbearably hot.

Then cool fabric was settling around her shoulders. "Frances." Her name on Duke's lips was as hot as her face. And her formerly queasy stomach now seemed to be doing a joyful little dance inside her. Neither sensation should have been pleasant, so why did she reach up to clench the newly draped coat tighter against her skin?

Because it smelled like Duke, that's why. Like air just after a storm breaks combined with the faintest hint of sun-warmed blackberries. Another coat was folded across his arm—Cyrus's?—but the one touching her neck clearly belonged to Duke.

"Won't Cyrus be cold without his coat?" she asked to fill the loaded silence. Well, that and to steady herself from the thrumming *something* pulsing through her veins.

Duke shook his head and she noted at last what she hadn't earlier. There were other clothes over his arm also. Enough to suggest Cyrus was now as naked as Duke. Or—

"He's a wolf too?"

Rather than nodding, Duke asked a question of his own. "Do you want me to walk you back to the hotel tonight?"

A lady would have said yes. But Frances instead disentangled the blackberry twig from her dress while reconsidering the shack's amenities. There was a homemade broom leaning against one wall, which would clean a spot sufficiently to lie down on. Duke's coat would make a quite adequate blanket. And even though a lady should never sleep with a strange man beside her, there was no rule of etiquette that forbade her from sharing body heat with a wolf.

Still, her tongue tangled up when she tried to say that. "I... Um... You..."

"Tell me what you want."

His blue eyes untangled her tongue and she found herself saying, "I want to stay here tonight. With your wolf."

She woke to heat deep inside her body. As if she'd been hugged all night by a man rather than simply pressing her side up against a wolf and sinking cold fingers into its fur.

On the other hand, the shack looked worse in daylight than it had the previous evening. Spiderwebs dangled from the rafters. The gaps between planks were large enough for snakes to slither in through. And Frances reached for the wolf to reassure herself that she wasn't alone.

Her fingers found nothing. The wolf—Duke—was gone.

Her breath came a little too fast as she slid back into her boots, the only item she'd removed the previous evening. In her haste, she mis-laced the first one and muttered a curse her father would very much have disapproved of. Then she stilled as male voices carried in from outside.

"He's been gone two days, you think? Three? More?"

That was Duke and the fear that had hastened Frances's fingers loosened. This time, she had no problem looping laces around grommets. Still, she paused to listen after tying the first knot.

"I don't know," Cyrus answered, frustration edging his reply. "I can't find his trail. And the letter…"

"We'll find him and we'll break the curse." Duke's words were a promise Frances could feel in her belly. "We'll start with his journal."

"The journal makes no sense!"

Finishing the laces, Frances came to her feet and found the journal on the table where the letter had been. This was none of her concern either, but Frances flipped through its pages anyway.

What she found there made the object seem more like a sketchbook than a journal. Ink outlined mountain landscapes, not in the form of a map but as if the artist had wanted to capture observed beauty. On the next page, two wolves ran together in joyful abandon. After that came a woman's face, young and beautiful. Louisa?

The final drawing was different. This image was so dark it seemed as if James had cross-hatched in a frenzy, creating a featureless emptiness fading to paler gray at the edges.

Frances had to agree with Cyrus. Unless Duke intended to use the landscapes to try to find specific locations, she didn't see how this journal would help track down what sounded like a missing friend.

Which was when she noticed the blackberry twig she'd set in a metal cup of water on the edge of the table last night. Then, a flower had rested at the end of the twig. Today, the tip bent down under the weight of a fruit.

The blackberry was as big as a crabapple, its ebony so intense it soaked up the sunlight. And suddenly Frances was starving. Her mouth watered and before she could stop herself, she reached out, plucked the berry, then popped it into her mouth.

Chapter 4

When Duke had left her alone fifteen minutes earlier, Frances was wrapped up in his coat and sound asleep. She'd looked so soft and kissable that it had taken an effort for him to turn away rather than waking her. But duty—and his brother—called. He was head of his pack. He was honor bound to respond.

Still, walking back through the door now, he smiled in anticipation. Chances were, Frances would still be curled up like a squirrel inside her nest. Perhaps he'd have a moment to lie back down beside her. Perhaps she'd lean into him the way she had last night. Perhaps her fingers would twine just as willingly into his hair as they had into his wolf's fur...

But he'd guessed wrong. Frances now stood beside the table upon which James's journal lay open. As if she'd flipped through its pages, something a stranger with no knowledge of the curse was unlikely to do.

Worse was the blackberry. It had been green and hard when he brushed past it moments earlier. Now, though, the fruit slid soft and ripe between her lips.

"Stop!" Duke demanded, not sure who he was protecting. His brother? Frances?

She paid him no mind, almost as if she hadn't heard him. Instead, she swallowed and the unmistakable tang of magic suffused the air inside the prospector's shack. Tropical flowers and vinegar, the combination unbearable for two very different reasons.

Duke clenched his fist against twin urges to stroke his fingers through Frances's tresses and to cast her over the nearest cliff. Because his guess in the stagecoach had been right.

She was fae. Was she also linked to his family curse?

Then the object of his admiration and fury was turning the journal around until it lay catty-corner to where it had been originally. The book was James's attempt to bypass the curse's twisting of any words written against it. If James had tried to pen a description of what he'd found while hunting the curse's source, every word would have turned bitter like those in the letter from Louisa.

So he'd left them a message in the form of pictures instead. Pictures that, as Cyrus had said, made absolutely no sense.

To them at least. Frances, in contrast, poked her finger at a bit of blackness surrounded by much more blackness. "Here," she murmured. "West."

Behind him, Cyrus growled. Of course he growled. Never mind the oddity of Frances understanding a message that had meant nothing to the two of them. Worse was the fact that the scent of the curse they'd spent weeks trying to break now permeated the inside of the prospector's shack.

So why did Duke take a step toward the source of the aroma that had caused his family so much heartache? "What's west?" he asked, keeping his voice quiet.

Frances's eyelids fluttered as if she was having trouble focusing. "James," she said after a long moment of silence. "The man who drew this. He's in the mountains near Dead Man's Pass."

"She couldn't possibly know that." Cyrus pushed himself the rest of the way through the doorway, filled the prospector's shack to bursting. It was no wonder Frances cringed back.

"Give her space," Duke demanded.

"You can't be serious," Cyrus countered. "Are you listening to yourself? We've lost enough to the…"

Duke silenced his brother with a hand over his mouth and a shove out the door, a mirror image of their behavior yesterday only without the rough contact with Frances that had raised Duke's hackles. Once they were twice as far away as they'd been the previous evening, he finally let Cyrus speak.

And, true to form, Cyrus had cooled down in the interim. "You can't intend to go off on a wild-goose chase while James is missing," he argued, choosing each word carefully. "It would take all morning to run to Dead Man's Pass in lupine form."

Now Duke was the one who bit off his syllables as if he was a wolf warning another away from his dinner. "I don't intend to run there as a wolf."

Cyrus shook his head. "Of course you don't. Let me guess. You intend to walk there the long, slow way. On two legs. Taking her with you."

The implication was clear. Frances had enchanted him.

And maybe she had. Still— "You need to trust my instincts, brother. Yours are twisted by the curse."

Predictably, heat rose in Cyrus's voice again. "*I'm* the one with twisted instincts? She's fae. You can smell it on her."

That part was true, but there was another part that was even more true. "She's also," Duke murmured, "my mate."

He made sure Frances ate before they left the prospector's shack. Rabbit grilled on a spit over an open fire shouldn't have appealed to a fae woman who likely subsisted on the finest of delicacies—aged wines, decadent pastries, and other luxuries fit for a queen. Yet Frances dug into their meager repast eagerly, and her hum of pleasure as she stripped meat from rabbit bones soothed Duke.

He was in dire need of soothing. Because Cyrus had decided to stay behind, searching for the pack mate they both had cause to worry over. After that pronouncement, Cyrus had gone silent. He did no more than shake his head when Duke promised, "We'll be back by nightfall tomorrow."

Duke couldn't explain in a way his brother would understand why he was following this fae woman he'd met only the day before up into the mountains. He couldn't explain it to Cyrus and he couldn't explain it to himself. Not beyond that simple word:

Mate.

Mate meant everything, though. Or it would if the curse was broken.

So he let Frances lead the way, trying not to be overwhelmed by suspicions when she sought out game trails with wolf-like ease. Together, they threaded between sheer cliffs and steep scree slopes, her confidence never flagging despite multiple splitting paths.

And all the while, she clutched that same blackberry twig, a twig that appeared to have grown larger while Duke wasn't looking. Only magic could have made the end he'd whittled off the main bush bulge and begin sending out tiny roots.

"You don't trust me." Frances's words carried back over her shoulder several hours later, the first words they'd shared since setting off other than warnings about uneven ground and other hazards.

"I trust my instincts." And his instincts continued to be harshly divided. On the one hand, Cyrus's assertions made rational sense. On the other hand, even though storm clouds were beginning to cast the landscape around them into deep shadow, Duke had no urge to turn back.

"Last night, you asked me why I was following you," Frances said as she hoisted herself over a boulder almost too large for her small limbs to wrap around. Even that awkward maneuver was managed with unearthly grace and Duke forced himself to look away.

"I couldn't answer the question to your satisfaction," she continued, "but I can tell you why I borrowed my maid's dress and left my father's hotel yesterday. I wanted an adventure. Independence. When I saw you in the stagecoach, I found what I'd craved."

Duke's wolf woke inside him. *He* was what she craved. That was right. That was proper. His mate...

Tamping down his simple, animal desires, Duke focused on what Frances wasn't telling him. "Your father. What's he like?"

"He's a potent force."

Potent. The word made Duke growl: "Did he hurt you?"

Frances laughed by way of reply, and Duke would have given anything to bask in that laughter forever. It flowed across him like a cascade of spring water, seeping into his pores as if fulfilling a desperate thirst. He barely took in what she said after that, focusing primarily on the assertion that she'd never come close to being hurt.

"Far from it. Father fulfilled my every whim. I once joked about wanting a partridge in a pear tree for Christmas and I woke the next morning to the most astonishing bird atop the tiniest tree imaginable. Did you know bonsais can bear fruit?"

If the fae asked it to, a tree pruned down to survive in a pot the size of his cupped palms would definitely bear fruit. "You didn't find that surprising?" Duke asked, choosing his words carefully.

"Of course I did! And I also didn't. Father works miracles." Frances shrugged as if this evidence of fae magic was par for the course.

Meanwhile, a blackberry root elongated and twined all the way around her forearm. Could Frances really be so oblivious to the magic dancing around her that she missed even this sign of the unworldly? Or was she hiding her true nature the way werewolves did while walking amid humans?

"You saw my wolf," Duke reminded her, testing his hypothesis. "Is your father a potent force like that?"

"Nothing like that," she started. "He's just..."

Then she went silent as they curved around another rock outcropping and saw before them the dark entrance to a cave.

Chapter 5

Ever since she bit down on that blackberry, the world had seemed different to Frances. Brighter, louder. As if she'd spent her entire life wrapped up in a fog bank that wind had abruptly whipped away.

Even her emotions were brighter and louder. Or that's how it felt as she stepped into the cave, already buffeted by the push and pull of Duke's interest in and doubt of her. Damp seeped out of the rough stone walls while a deeper darkness coiled in the furthest corner.

No, that wasn't darkness. That was a wolf, sprawled across the irregular dirt floor as if he was dead.

"James!" Duke sprinted toward his fallen friend even as the air electrified. The blackberry twig twitched between Frances's fingers, and she turned in the direction it bade her to find a dark figure materializing out of thin air just inside the entrance.

Her father was a man of imposing stature, dressed in a long black coat and boasting an authoritative stance that demanded attention. Physically, he looked exactly the same as she remembered. But how had she failed to notice the calculation glinting within his dark eyes?

"Well done, my dear," Father said in a voice that sent shivers down her spine. "The wolves sought to break free of us, but you drew their leader directly into my grasp. You've made me proud."

Out of the corner of her eye, she saw Duke jerking his attention up from the wolf in his arms, the wolf that was now feverishly paddling its paws against thin air. At least James wasn't dead. But Frances had intended to help him, not harm him. She'd certainly wanted nothing to do with drawing Duke into a trap.

When she opened her mouth to say as much, however, no words came out. Instead, Duke was the one who spoke.

"Us?" he repeated, those vivid blue eyes boring into Frances even as he spoke to her father. "There was no *us* in your depredations. Frances is too young to have been part of my family's curse."

"Is that so?" Father raised one eyebrow. "You seem to be operating under multiple misapprehensions. First, there is no curse—simply a bargain your father and I made between us. And since you're the result of that bargain, perhaps you should refrain from telling me my own business."

Again, Frances opened her mouth to speak and again her tongue twisted itself up into silence. Her hand clenched down on the blackberry twig, this time so hard a thorn pressed into her palm without quite piercing the skin.

The clarity that had suffused her since swallowing the blackberry was fading. And something about the returning muddle suggested...

"Now," her father said, stepping closer to Frances and breaking her train of thought, "let's make you presentable."

With a flick of his wrist, he spun her simple maid's dress away, replacing it with a gown that sparkled like stars in the heavens. Her hair—unbrushed after waking amid mouse droppings that morning—twisted itself up into the most elegant chignon. The scent of frangipani and orchids enfolded her, but Frances felt no tingle of astonishment at her own transformation.

Instead, it was as if a cloud had engulfed her entire being. Was this muggy emptiness really how she'd lived her entire life until this morning? Only the memory of Duke's wide smile prevented her from succumbing entirely to the undertow.

While Frances was struggling to get her brain on track, Father snapped his fingers and this time Duke was the one affected. Dropping his friend into the dirt with none of the gentleness he'd displayed earlier, Duke started toward Frances. Darkness behind his eyes proved that his forward momentum was not of his own choosing.

"You thought you could renounce our bargain," Father mused as Duke's cheek twitched with the effort to slow his advance. "But what you failed to understand is that *you* are the bargain. Your father wanted sons and he got two of them. There is no way to take that back. Now remove the briar from my daughter's hand and destroy it."

Duke couldn't stop himself from walking toward her. But unlike Frances, he hadn't lost his voice.

"I know you think your father is kind," he said, words forceful yet even as if he was managing them as carefully as he managed his footsteps. "But he cursed my bloodline. Our mates reject us. As soon as my mother gave birth to me and Cyrus, she fled the pack and our father followed. We've seen neither of them since."

Frances didn't need convincing. Despite the fog dulling her senses, she understood her father much more clearly now than she ever had before.

He'd used her in the past and was using her now. *She* was somehow integral to this curse, even though she didn't understand the specifics of it. Father was sucking something out of her, something that made her head dull and her tongue tangle. That same something, if she didn't miss her guess, was what allowed him to bend Duke to his will.

And Duke *was* bending. Outside, a crash of thunder suggested the storm clouds had finally opened, but she could still hear the steady thud of Duke's feet as he advanced toward her. Meanwhile, the cave interior grew brighter rather than dimmer as light pulsed off her father in waves.

"When Louisa came into our lives," Duke said, taking another step forward, "we thought perhaps the curse applied only to our parents' generation. But her pregnancy—" his breath caught, his eyes closing as if he couldn't bear to look at past events and also couldn't stop himself from doing so "—it woke up the curse. She plans to leave our pack and the child as soon as it's born."

A pain twisted just where Duke's child must lie within Louisa and Frances lost track of the glimmer of understanding that had been starting to break through the muffling clouds. How had she allowed herself to read so much into behavior that was merely gentlemanly? The over-wide smile, the cliff-side rescue, the borrowed coat, the warmth of fur last night. None of that had meant anything if Louisa was Duke's wife.

Frances swallowed and her father chuckled. Then he spoke, speeding along Duke's story even as he snapped his fingers and sped up Duke's footsteps. "So you sought a way to break our bargain. You learned about my weakness and crossed the country to root it out."

Frances was her father's weakness? If so, she could stop this. And she would. Because despite her disappointment with regard to Duke's intentions, she wasn't about to let Father harm the man who had been nothing but kind.

Again she opened her mouth. Again, nothing came out.

And now Duke was so close his hands could wrap themselves around hers. Rough-skinned yet gentle in manner, they enclosed her chill in such warmth she wanted to cry.

That warmth belonged to Louisa. Duke's words, however, were intended only for Frances.

"It's okay. You can give me the twig. We have the rest of the bush back at the cabin."

Wait—her father's weakness was the blackberry bush, not his daughter? Then why did it feel like energy was being channeled out of Frances to force Duke to bend to her father's will?

Perhaps there was more to the story. Perhaps that fairy tale her nursemaid told her hadn't been such a fairy tale.

And when Duke stared into her eyes with lupine intensity, a little bit of the cloud lifted. The tale that had sprung clear and full into her mind as the blackberry slid down her throat that morning bubbled back up in her nursemaid's words.

There'd been a girl born to a fae father and a human mother. A girl whose existence was fueled by a bargain.

A girl doomed to fall into an enchanted sleep if ever a thorn pricked her finger. And if Frances wasn't her father's weakness, was actually his strength...

The fog came down hard again, trying to consume her. But Frances wouldn't let it. Instead, she clenched her fist as tight as she could around the thorn digging into her palm.

It wasn't enough. And she couldn't speak to ask for help. All she could do was stare into Duke's vivid blue eyes and hope he'd understand...

He did. He squeezed. Squeezed her hand tight around a thorny twig that, at last, bit through her skin and drew blood.

Chapter 6

She fell through Duke's fingers. One moment she was warm and alert in front of him. The next, she'd dropped like a stone into a still pond...or rather, toward the hard cave floor.

He tried to catch her. But unlike on that cliff edge, he hadn't expected the fall. And this time the danger was more than broken bones.

No wonder his wolf reacted, ripping out of his skin and his clothes and his mind and growling as the evil that was her father approached Frances's crumpled form. If he'd killed her...

Frances wasn't dead. Only sleeping, her breath warm against the sensitive skin of Duke's nostrils. Meanwhile, her father seemed to be having a fit, if a fit involved waving his hands and snapping his fingers. Frustration twisted his features and for the first time a trace of humanity crept into his expression. "Obey me!" he demanded.

Duke had no urge to do the old man's bidding. Which meant, with magic no longer dragging at his muscles and with Frances in no immediate peril, now would be a good time to rip out the old man's throat.

Only Frances's presence stopped Duke from taking out the potential threat before it could become more than potential. She'd be horrified to wake to her father's bloody corpse in front of her.

Duke refused to consider the fact that she might not wake.

Unfortunately, he'd read a great quantity of fairy stories while trying to figure out how to break the curse that had broken his family. One had involved a spindle pricking a finger rather than a thorn piercing a palm, but the sleep that resulted had seemed much like this one.

And that sleep had lasted a hundred years.

It had also been broken by true love's kiss. Something Duke just happened to be perfectly equipped to offer.

Before his lips could meet Frances's, however, he had to shift. Unfolding upward into naked humanity, he caught the moment realization dawned on the old man's face. "The bargain," Frances's father muttered. "It's broken."

Wait...what? Duke had thought the old man's strength had simply run dry. "If the curse is broken, why is Frances sleeping?"

"I *told* you." As Frances's father spoke, his limbs gnarled like the roots of a tree that had been forced to contort itself into rocky crevices. If Duke wasn't mistaken, the man before him was much older than he had initially appeared.

"Tell me again," Duke suggested, trying to focus on his original purpose but finding it nearly impossible with Frances's lips one inch from his. The scent of orchids lay heady between them and he was no longer torn between two wishes. He knew precisely what he wanted to do.

He forced himself to wait, however. Forced himself to merely breathe her breath while her father spoke as if to himself.

"I craved a way to work magic in the human realm," the old man said, his voice growing more musical and otherworldly by the moment, "and your father craved sons. The bargain allowed for Frances's conception and for yours also. There was no curse. Only a bargain upon which we both agreed."

The curse involved *Frances's* conception as well as his and Cyrus's? Facts Duke had been avoiding dwelling on now coalesced in his mind.

Frances biting into the blackberry that morning, the faint aura of magic around her exploding at the exact same moment. The old man's power splintering when Frances fell into an enchanted sleep.

She was the curse? The tangled knot at the center of this magical mess?

Pack forgive him, Duke wanted to kiss her anyway.

"The bargain let me grant my darling daughter gowns and jewels," her father continued. "I took excellent care of her! Treated her like the most precious of gifts!"

"Which was never what she wanted," Duke murmured, considering the woman in his arms. Frances had discarded all of the trappings of wealth except for her entirely sensible boots while escaping on her adventure. If his guesses were correct, she'd never wanted anything from her father other than love the fae being seemed incapable of providing.

Because Frances's father wasn't watching his daughter's torso the way Duke was, counting breaths and trying to decide whether they were slowing. Instead, the older man was turning over his own hands, wailing as moss sprang up in the creases of his knuckles. "I'm of the earth but this earth won't dance for me any longer!" He stamped one foot like a child lost in the throes of a tantrum.

Frances's father cared only for Frances's father. Which meant he likely wasn't lying about one thing—Frances really was the so-called bargain, or rather the axis around which Duke's family curse revolved.

As long as Frances slept, Duke's family would stay safe. Louisa wouldn't flee their pack. Perhaps Duke's parents might even find their way back home and back to each other.

But Duke couldn't leave the woman he loved consumed by an enchanted sleep. Not when Cyrus still possessed the bulk of the blackberry bush, a way to save the pack if waking Frances had the unfortunate side effect of refreshing her father's powers.

It should have been a case of the good of many weighed against the good of one. But Frances wasn't just one. She was his mate.

The wolf didn't give Duke time to finish working the problem. Instead, it dipped his head down and kissed Frances on the lips.

Chapter 7

Frances woke to blackberry on her tongue and the distant sound of her father crowing his triumph. She knew that was bad. She knew it, but all she could focus on was the warmth spilling through her, pooling deep within her belly. The way Duke's grip on her chin felt like liquid sunlight, how the softness of his lips contrasting with the roughness of emerging whiskers made her feel more alive than she'd ever felt in her life.

The enchanting aroma of blackberry flooded her senses and she eased open her mouth to take in more of it. Then her father's stark command broke the moment like a glass shattering against stone.

"Remove the briar from my daughter's hand *now*."

Duke relinquished his hold on her chin more gently than he'd dropped James's lupine body. But, despite his care, he couldn't resist her father. He twisted the twig out from between her fingers, unwinding roots she hadn't even realized were growing around her arm.

"St—" Frances couldn't manage a single syllable before her tongue tangled within her mouth. And she understood now where that tangle originated.

From her father. It was his way of keeping her under control.

She couldn't speak, but her body was still her own. And she'd heard what was happening while she drifted in semi-slumber.

Her father had used her to harm Duke's family. The blackberry twig was the way to break that stranglehold.

A solution Duke had chosen not to take advantage of, perhaps due to concern about sending her back into an enchanted sleep. Frances, however, had no such compunction. Not now that she'd seen who her father really was.

The trick would be to keep him from noticing what she was up to. Which, honestly, shouldn't be terribly difficult. Her father never had noticed her unless he wanted an ornament to grace his arm or salon.

"One more kiss," she murmured, trying to sound as ornamental as possible. "Please, Father. Let me kiss Duke one last time…"

The words came out easily now. Perhaps because her craving to taste Duke was so powerful. Or, more likely, because her father considered her weak and her craving seemed like further weakness.

It wasn't, however. The craving was Frances's greatest strength.

For a moment, she thought the ruse would fail. But then her father shrugged and replied, "If you must." He'd used the same tone in the past when granting her wonders she now realized had been born out of her own magic, the energy fueling the spell stolen from Duke and from his family.

Fury spun through her like the prick of the briar. But she kept her face smooth as she took the two steps to return herself to Duke's proximity. She grasped his arm as if steadying herself in preparation for going up on tiptoes to reach his lips.

She didn't kiss him though. Instead, she scraped a hole into the dirt of the cave floor with one toe as if bashful. "Turn around, Father," she murmured. "Please?"

She thought she'd overdone the meek-and-mild act for a moment, but her father had always wanted her to be a porcelain doll. Beautiful and lacking in volition. Now, he saw precisely what she wanted him to see.

He turned. And in the moment when her father's eyes were averted, Frances snatched the twig out of Duke's hand, thrusting long roots into the hole she'd dug for it. Then she patted soil back around its base and murmured: "Grow."

Magic was a wondrous thing. The tiny plant had been no more than a sprig in her hand yesterday, just as her acquaintance with Duke had been no more than an attraction to blue eyes and a wide smile.

Today, both magnified into something *more*.

The twig exploded into a thorny hedge, thorn-covered tendrils reaching and vining. It wanted her. It sought her...

Duke swept her out of the path of the wild floral abundance but her father had no such protection. Instead, he was pinned down by the blackberry, branches twining over his arms and legs, across his neck and head.

Her father fought back but with no effect. He and his magic were equally caged.

Happily ever afters are full of rodent bones and naked men and damp wolf fur. Or so Frances decided hours later, after her father had given up on beating himself against the confines of his verdant prison and had taken himself back to Faery. After James woke starving and Duke apologized for leaving her then ran four-legged out into the storm to hunt dinner for his weakened pack mate. After James shifted into a tall redhead whose face looked just like the woman in the sketchbook who Frances had somehow forgotten about.

"Louisa," Frances murmured, turning away from the fire James was building near the mouth of the cave. Perhaps smoke would explain the sudden tears stinging her eyes. "She's your sister?"

"Yes." James was shivering even inside Duke's clothing. Even with the addition of the coat Frances had shed—also Duke's, when it came right down to it. He was so close to the fire that she could smell wool singeing, but James's body still shook so violently that his voice shook too when he continued. "Louisa can go back to her mate now. She'll be eternally in your debt."

"She owes me nothing," Frances answered. Now that she knew she was half-fae, she supposed she could gather debts like funds in the bank. But she had no intention of falling into that trap.

Because she wasn't just fae; she was human also. And the human half of her came with a conscience that suggested even her father's ill-gotten earthly funds should be considered off limits. She'd need to return the money to its previous owners somehow. Find another way to survive.

While she was still thinking that through, Duke returned, shaking water out of his fur then dropping a dead ground squirrel at James's feet. After that, he came to sit beside Frances, head cocked as if he could smell the turmoil in her gut.

And maybe he could. But she didn't want to concern him when he had so many other troubles already, so she hastened to reassure him that she wouldn't be a burden. "In the morning, I'll see if I can find a position in the town where the stagecoach stops. I won't be your problem for more than one more night, I promise."

Which is when Duke flung himself upward into humanity. And even knowing he was Louisa's mate didn't prevent Frances from tracing the flicker of the campfire across the rain-slick muscles of his naked back.

She watched his back because he'd turned away from her in order to stalk toward James. "What did you say to Frances?" Duke demanded, each word full of fury Frances had never thought she'd hear on his usually cautious tongue.

"I told her Louisa would be in her debt," James answered, his voice even meeker than Frances's had been when facing her father. "Alpha, I apologize. I didn't mean to…"

Frances swallowed down something that tasted like tears, then she interceded. "James said nothing wrong. And you have more to worry about than me. If the curse really is broken, Louisa will want the father of her child close as soon as possible."

"Agreed," Duke murmured, the firelight on his angles even more beautiful as he turned back to face her. His wide mouth was so endlessly enticing, even clenched into a hard line rather than smiling. Frances wished she'd had time for more than a single half-asleep kiss.

"Cyrus will be ecstatic," Duke continued. "And I still have no idea why you think your presence is a *problem* to me."

"*Cyrus* will be ecstatic," Frances repeated, turning the conversations she'd heard over in her mind a second time and coming to a very different conclusion. Was it possible that—

"Yes," Duke agreed. "Louisa's mate will be ecstatic. Just as I hope to make mine."

⁂

Author's Note

Briar Moon began as a family story passed down from my mother's great grandfather. He'd traveled to California during the Gold Rush, my mother told me, backing up her story with a little leather pouch so soft it felt like fur between my fingers. "If you look inside very carefully, you might find a speck of gold dust."

I never did. And as I grew older, I became more interested in the second half of the story. My ancestor had brought home not only gold but also a blackberry bush which was planted in the family's yard and from which I'd eaten huge, delicious berries as a child. How fascinating, I thought, that my great, great grandfather had been so intrigued by this plant that he'd carted a thorny bush on what was, at that time, a difficult journey back to Massachusetts.

More recently, I started digging into the story further. Googling turned up a document from 1933 titled <u>The Shoe Industry in Weymouth</u> which contained the information that my ancestor happened to run a shoe factory in addition to having participated in the Gold Rush. The document included this intriguing paragraph:

Because most of the adventurers came home "broke," and as Prince Tirrell did not, he was asked how it happened that he annexed some of the yellow stuff? The characteristic explanation was, that quest for gold was something like a group of young people going out to pick berries. Many wander about seeking loaded bushes, and in the aggregate pick but a few; while others would patiently remain in a limited area, be contented with a moderate outlook, and as a result fill their buckets. Prince H. declared that in gold mining he stuck to a prospect and picked it clean.

Suddenly I wondered whether that storied blackberry bush my great-great-grandfather brought back had been real or had been a metaphor for his prospecting. And what other kinds of metaphorical gold might you find on such a journey?

That flight of fancy turned into this story. I hope you enjoyed the result!

Small Change

The coins clanked in the stranger's palm as he picked through them. I tapped my foot. Five minutes ago, we'd been caught in a freak thunderstorm that soaked my blazer and his dress jacket while we scurried for the safety of this empty laundromat. We struck a deal to pool our resources in the interest of leaving this place drier than we started. I had a quarter; one dryer run cost fifty cents.

"You don't have a quarter?" I asked.

He looked up from his coins at last, his eyes a shade of blue as rich as sky grading into ocean. His voice brought to mind long summer days when I'd lounged in the grass listening to wood thrushes, before college, before law school, before cases filled every waking moment.

"I have a Deutsch mark. I believe that's worth more than a fourth of an American dollar?"

For one split second, I was twelve years old again. Back when happiness had been a book and a dog and cookies for snacking wrapped by a loving parent. Back when I'd dreamed of traveling the world, of collecting coins from every nation I visited. Back when free time had been an invitation, not a fight.

Then my chilled fingers lost their grip on my briefcase. It slipped down, down, down and I barely caught the handle before it struck the pavement and split open.

I couldn't afford this distraction. And I definitely couldn't show up in court looking like this.

Impatience made my voice snap. "Germany uses euros now, and either way it's irrelevant. We're in the United States. You don't have a quarter?"

"I have a coin from a Roman villa stamped with the head of Julius Caesar as a youth. This, I think, would be worth more than the entire public wash house?"

"It's a laundromat," I corrected while berating myself for falling into the trap no lawyer should ever fall for—the supposedly well-meaning handshake deal.

It was time to get out of here and see if I could find a hairbrush and a replacement blazer in the seventeen minutes remaining before court went into session. Still, against my better judgment, I forced one last repeat of the only relevant question out through chattering teeth. "You don't have a quarter?"

"I don't have a quarter," the stranger agreed. Then he snapped his fingers and abruptly I was dry and warm, the sensation of being wrapped in a quilt straight off a sun-drenched clothesline enfolding not only my skin but everything underneath it.

Above me, puffy white clouds floated across a sky as blue as his eyes. And his voice wasn't the only music as he finished: "But I *can* grant your wish."

Second-generation Changeling

The old, blue pickup truck was running on fumes. Sibilan smiled wryly and sent a whisper of suggestion to the pint of gasoline sloshing about in the bottom of the tank. The fluid promptly obeyed her and doubled in size.

Twice nothing is still very nearly nothing, Sibilan reminded herself. But the gasoline would last until she got into town and back out again, or at least she hoped so. And once she left the concrete city, she could ask it to double again. After all, she was a second-generation changeling—purely human but with a splash of magic sufficient for the simplest of tasks.

Gas, however, was the least of her problems, as her adopted mother had pointed out when she left their tiny pocket of Faery that morning.

"I don't see why you want to go." Mami gestured at the beauty of forest-turned-garden. "If you're bored, invasive autumn olives are moving into the old field down valley. Haven't you felt them blocking the early spring ephemerals out?"

"Yes," Sibilan admitted. The dense shrub overwhelmed native plants and poisoned the soil so nothing else could grow up through it. A meadow vole had dropped by to chitter about the issue just that morning. Still: "I'm even more human than you are, Mami. I need to see where I came from."

Papi had appeared to be intent upon teasing the old willow into extending its graceful arch over their summer dining area, but now he joined the conversation even though he didn't open his eyes. "Are you worried about the upheaval at Court, Sibby-sweet? I thought you understood our home isn't really part of Faery. We just do our best to make it feel that way."

"I know," Sibilan answered. "I can't explain why I have to go, but I do. Will you tell me where you met my birth mother or won't you?"

They told her. They lent her the pickup they used on the rare occasions when purchased soil amendments proved an asset to their garden worth going out into the world for, they gave her their blessing, and they were so intent upon molding the willow together that they didn't even wave goodbye.

And that's how Sibilan came to be rolling into a human town for her first time ever, eyes wide as she peered at glowing signs taller than a tulip-tree along with vast expanses of concrete without a hint of greenery.

There was life present though. Stopping at a red light—something her mother had warned her about—she considered the man stepping out of one of the strange rectangular buildings. His plaid shirt over faded blue jeans was far from unusual, being the same outfit worn by half the folks in town. Yet something about this stranger drew her attention. Something reminiscent of the moment when the first spring migrant touched down on her palm after its long journey, feet so warm and tiny they made her heart take flight.

The harsh honk of a horn reminded Sibilan that time moved differently outside Faery. Green meant go and she was parked in the middle of a street, so she took her foot off the brake and rolled past the tantalizing stranger, ignoring the flash of green as his eyes rose to meet her own.

Yes, time moved differently outside Faery, even the little pocket of not-quite-Faery her parents managed. Which meant that the green-eyed man, despite appearing roughly her age, was likely several decades her junior.

Mortals bear children by the dozen, she reminded herself. *My birth parents will be old by now. Their kids will have had kids. He could be one of them...*

Sibilan shivered as the town's aura washed over her. Anger, pain, joy, confusion, and an overwhelming haze of tiredness. It all seeped into her bones, shoving away the serenity of the forest she'd left behind not long ago.

Sibilan had never felt more human than in that moment. She'd never before doubted her ability to complete her quest.

It was nearly noon by the time the pickup rolled to a stop behind the library. The end of the parking lot she chose was empty but it still took Sibilan three tries before she managed to get the vehicle situated between a set of painted lines. Parking, like many other mortal pursuits, was difficult for fae, even second-generation changelings like herself.

Still, she'd made it. Sliding down out of the metal and plastic contraption, she headed straight for a nearby patch of lawn and slipped out of her sandals so she could sink bare feet into lush vegetation. Relief eased her anxiety-induced tunnel vision and allowed her to consider her surroundings at last.

Despite the bustle elsewhere, no one was watching her now other than a tail-flicking squirrel. Good thing too since she wasn't dressed to blend, at least not yet. Unclasping her cloak of autumn leaves, she swirled it in the air, flipping the garment inside out.

Now she appeared to wear a wool cloak dyed a pale dirt-brown. Not an ordinary garment in this small Appalachian town, but less eye-catching than the glittering beauty her father had magicked together for her three autumns ago. Mortals wouldn't be able to see through the illusion, but the local wildlife was more keen-eyed.

A crow winged down to land on her shoulder and pick at the metal clasp with its beak. "Shh. Not now," Sibilan said softly. "I'm a mortal today. Remember that."

The bird bobbed its head once as if nodding, even though everyone knew bird head-bobs were courtship behavior. It was teasing her for doing the exact opposite of what any right-minded critter would do—covering up her most beautiful plumage.

"You don't understand humans," she murmured at its receding silhouette when the bird gave up on communication and flew into the blue sky above her. "And neither do I."

Still, the library was a solid lead, a spot Mami had promised doled out information to anyone and everyone. "You came from a small town," Mami had told her during one of her long-ago bedtime stories. "Everyone knows everyone there. That's why your birth mother put you up for adoption. She didn't want to be stigmatized as a teenage mother for the rest of her life."

"But a mortal only remains a teenager for a few short years," Sibilan had countered, not understanding.

Mami shrugged, turning away from her daughter to ease a sticky seed coat off a cotyledon on one of the hepaticas on the windowsill. "I can't say I understand mortal impulses. Her name, before you ask, is Jill Pointer. We found her through the local library. They know everything in a small town."

So Sibilan stepped into the dark concrete building with a single goal—finding Jill Pointer. And to her surprise, the task proved easier than she'd expected. All she had to do was say her birth mother's name, although that part wasn't particularly easy. The mere speaking made her tremble like the last maple leaf clinging to a twig before being brushed free by an autumn wind.

But the librarian's face crumpled into kindly wrinkles in response. "Oh dear. I'm so sorry, honey. Jill died thirty years ago. But she's still got kin in town."

Behind Sibilan, the library doors gusted open, billowing out Sibilan's cloak and setting the leaves rustling. But the inside-out glamour appeared to do its job because the librarian didn't comment upon its oddity. Instead, she smiled over Sibilan's shoulder as if she'd spirited a relative out of the autumn day just by wishing for it. "In fact, here's one of them now. Jill's son—Dylan."

Sibilan turned slowly, knowing who she would see. It was the green-eyed man who'd made her heart leap at the red light. His grin did more than that, striking her like lightning out of a cloudless sky.

"Looking for me?" asked the man who was her brother.

Dylan had to be much younger than Sibilan's actual age, but he appeared a year or two older by mortal standards. Both of his arms were decorated with swirling tattoos she couldn't quite make out from a distance and Sibilan didn't realize she was staring until he spoke.

"Wanna see?" He rolled up his sleeves further to reveal arms that rippled with muscle and ink and...

Sibilan swallowed. This was her *brother*. He shared half of her genetics. She wasn't a member of the Unseelie Court. She toed moral lines.

"No thank you," she told him, averting her eyes from the temptation. "I'm working on an oral-history project about my family. Your family. Our family."

She was running at the mouth like the brook after a deluge, leaping over the banks and forgetting her original path. Remembering Papi's ability to focus during windstorms, she took a deep breath and re-centered. "I'm your distant cousin, several times removed. I'm trying to learn about your mother, Jill Pointer."

Dylan weighed the story, one eyebrow raised, before shrugging. "Better take you to meet her sister then. I don't remember my mom, but Aunt Annie does."

Which is where they went. Across town with him leading the way in a vehicle that didn't spit out fumes like her truck did—perhaps her parents needed to consider an upgrade? She did her best to focus on the rules of the road rather than the fact that her birth mother was dead and her brother was hotter than exposed clifftops at summer noon. The confusion in her gut felt like earthworms churning up the soil when it was time to plant.

But earthworms were helpful. Her confusion wasn't. *I didn't come here to meet Dylan Pointer,* she reminded herself. She'd come out of an odd sort of discontent with her world, regardless of its peace and beauty. She'd come searching for something and maybe that something was an understanding about the family who'd produced her. An understanding about who she was beneath the cloak she'd turned inside-out to blend in.

So when Dylan drew up at the curb in front of a house half swallowed by ivy, she inhaled relief. This place, she could understand. This place made sense.

The people inside did not. There were so many. Aunt Annie and her husband John. A grown cousin of Dylan's with her own husband and what seemed like an uncountable number of offspring. Another cousin with even more youngsters in tow. The children flitted through the house like tiny birds banding together to seek winter forage and Sibilan lost track of their names the moment they were voiced.

By the time the clock on the wall—such an oddity, counting minutes—had turned its larger hand twice around the circle, she was so exhausted she was swaying. Aunt Annie had run through a cascade of family stories that eroded Sibilan's composure as if she was soft stone beneath a waterfall. She'd come here for this...and she couldn't take another moment of it.

"And Jill never did manage to get pregnant again so she adopted Dylan."

The words broke through the cloud that had padded Sibilan from the relentless cascade of sound. Her gaze shot to the man who'd spent all this time leaning against the doorway. Not quite in, not quite out. He wasn't her blood brother after all, but his words were fraternal when he finally spoke.

"She's exhausted, Aunt Annie."

"Why, so she is! Do you have a place to stay while you're in town?"

"Well, I..." Sibilan had meant to say that she'd booked a room at a hotel, but she realized just in time that she hadn't seen a single establishment of that type in her drive down Main Street. Still, she couldn't imagine sleeping in this house that looked so calm on the outside but felt like it hosted an entire colony of gnomes.

So she'd go home. Mami and Papi would welcome her back with open arms and the autumn olives really did need evicting. Why did that churning in her belly pick up speed at the mere thought of turning tail and going back the way she'd come?

"She's staying with me," Dylan interjected.

"In your mom's old place?" Aunt Annie frowned. "She'll fall through the floor and…"

"The kitchen is usable. I just finished the downstairs bedroom this morning but I haven't moved out of the attic yet. She can sleep there."

"Women need toilets, sinks, bathtubs."

"If one of each is acceptable, I can meet those needs."

The whole situation should have been awkward. But the peace of Dylan's home enfolded Sibilan the moment she stepped in the door and took in unexpected touches of artisanal beauty. Wood molding was carved so the natural grain morphed into landscapes. Walls were painted the color of foggy meadows. And windows, so many windows, brought the outside in.

Despite the way his work spoke all around him, Dylan himself was tight-lipped. He just handed her a towel and toothbrush then told her which rooms to stay out of for her own safety. She didn't really listen because she didn't feel like exploring. Instead, she slept more soundly than she had in weeks.

The morning sun woke Sibilan long before anyone else in the neighborhood was stirring. She slipped out of bed and wrapped her cloak firmly around her, wool side out. Then she tiptoed through the living room that, in daylight, had clearly been repurposed as a carpenter's workshop. Was that what Dylan did? Build things?

No, he flipped houses. She remembered that now from Annie's chatter. The image that had popped into her head and out of her mouth in response made the older woman laugh so hard tears had sprung into her eyes. "Dylan fixes up run-down houses then sells them," Aunt Annie had clarified. And maybe that's what he was doing with this house as well? Fixing up the home their mother had let fall into disrepair before turning it over to a family who would fill it up with children dancing around each other like quarreling fox cubs?

Sibilan wasn't sure why the thought gave her such a pang.

Outside, then. The natural world always made her feel better.

Feet on grass, she stopped walking and breathed in the morning. It was just past dawn and the birds were already searching for their breakfast. Next door, the flame-colored leaves beneath a sugar maple had been carefully raked into a pile. The result was irresistible, the scent of damp and decomposing chlorophyll carrying easily to her nose.

Worries fled as Sibilan took a running leap and fell into beauty. Maple leaves frolicked around her and she let them boost her up onto a horizontal limb where she perched, dangling feet tickled by the last few leafy dancers.

Beneath her, the pile was no longer a pile despite mortals' efforts to bring order to autumnal chaos. Well, she wouldn't be the one to steal the illusion of control from this human neighborhood. Winter would do that job soon enough.

"Back you go," she whispered, and the leaves giggle-rustled as they obeyed, retreating into their pile.

Her thoughts weren't as easily ordered. She'd come to this mortal enclave seeking connection to her birth family and had found only differences. Seven children in Aunt Annie's house under the age of ten and their parents little more than children themselves. She shivered—to a fairy, a child was a vast responsibility to be taken on at maturity, maybe once or twice in a lifetime. Her parents had chosen to adopt her only when they themselves passed the two-century mark.

"Sibilan."

She swiveled in alarm as Dylan's voice carried across the lawn. She'd meant to be long gone when her brother—*adopted brother*, she corrected herself—came looking for his house guest. She couldn't decide what he thought of her or what she thought of him but she had the sneaking suspicion Dylan had taken her home out of pity, the same way her parents housed motherless bunnies then let the youngsters hop away again without bothering to give them names.

She'd intended to hop away herself before Dylan could muster the energy to shoo her out the door this morning. And she certainly hadn't meant to be caught sitting up in a maple tree, to be stared at by a silent man who embodied mystery.

But here beneath the gentle sun of morning, Dylan seemed warmer, as if the blankets he'd cocooned himself in overnight still left their imprint in places other than the sharp cheekbones above his slightly stubbled jaw. His green eyes also seemed sharper than she'd given them credit for yesterday. He'd surely notice if she jumped down without marring the leaf pile below her. For the first time in her extensive trunk-climbing experience, Sibilan was trapped up a tree.

"You have a chickadee on your shoulder," Dylan said conversationally as he reached the edge of that leaf pile.

"Oh." Sibilan twisted her head to consider the cheeky bird. *Shoo!* She thought at it. *Do you want the mortal to realize I'm fae?*

It sat there for one long moment then flew off, dee-dee-deeing mischievously. "I guess I was sitting still for a while," Sibilan said, trying to cover up the distinctly un-mortal-like behavior. "I was meditating."

Meditating, Papi had once told her, could be used to explain away all sorts of fae lapses.

Dylan only smiled and extended those tattooed arms up toward her. This close, she could see that the twining ink created a forest of leaves and birds and flowers. "I'll help you down," he offered. "Wouldn't want to ruin Mrs. Brown's leaf pile."

Sibilan flushed but she saw no alternative. So she let her body slip into his grasp, his large hands cupping her hips and sending fire shimmering through every nerve ending.

She was breathless when her feet settled onto the earth at last. And she wasn't the only one affected. This close, she could see Dylan's pulse fluttering hard and fast at the base of his throat.

"So you're researching your family, eh?" He said after the longest moment in history. He flicked her cloak and it opened just the tiniest fraction, flashing fae beauty out into the mortal world.

Had he noticed? Sibilan figured the best defense was a good offense. "Did *you* ever go in search of your birth parents?" she countered.

"Mine weren't...accessible."

And that's when she saw it. The absurd color of his eyes that had captured her from the beginning. They weren't the muddy hazel that mortals called green, were they? More like emeralds illuminated from within.

His stillness in the storm of his adopted family wasn't mortal stillness either. Plus, the carvings, the tattoos. Both were a craving.

As a mortal raised by first-generation changelings, Sibilan understood that craving. Or the flip side of it maybe.

This time, when a crow landed on her shoulder and bobbed its head, she didn't beg it to take flight like the chickadee. This time, when Dylan's green eyes saw deeper into her than she'd intended anyone in this town to see, she didn't change the subject.

Instead, she offered something she'd never considered offering. "Perhaps you'd like to see where you came from?" she offered, understanding at last what had drawn her to leave her home.

A Snowball's Chance

Chapter 1

I only realized I was stalking a six-year-old when a snowflake landed in my eye. Biting at the ice embedded in my foot pad, I forced myself into the present. Gradually, the olfactory memory of blood faded into the reality of stale slush.

The trouble was, the six-year-old looked like a fairy. Not because of her rainbow tutu stretching across a puffy pink snowsuit. And not because of the unicorn-shaped barrette holding back her bangs.

She looked like a fairy because of the way she danced through the snowy forest tapping laden tree limbs one after another. "Rise, majesty!" she crowed as a flurry of white cascaded down, barely missing her upturned face. Released from its weight, the branch snapped skyward, allowing the fairy to dance underneath.

I shivered, only partly because of the cold I'd never experienced before this winter. Fae were full of graceful beauty...and casual cruelty. I knew because I was one.

Half fae. Half wolf. Half human. I'm well aware that's too many halves to be contained within one being. But when the Queen of the Unseelie Court slept with a werewolf twenty-five years ago, I was what the pair of them conceived.

Now, I tried to turn away from the human child only to find my paws curving back in her direction. The high-pitched giggles were infectious. Not dangerously seductive like a fae laugh, but full of innocent joy I'd never experienced before.

What could possibly be funny about raising your hood for warmth and instead sending a cascade of frigid snow down the back of your neck? I couldn't imagine, but the girl's lips curled upward at the experience. I craved to understand.

So I followed her, even though I had an appointment elsewhere. I followed her despite having learned the hard way that I couldn't stride unscathed through werewolf territory...and nearly everywhere on this earth turned out to be werewolf territory. I should have been slinking, scenting for danger. Instead, I padded closer while a miniature human sang to the pines.

"Beautiful tree, higher than the sun! Bring me rainbow juice, yum, yum, yum!"

The child had no idea that juice squeezed from rainbows was used to loosen tongues and reveal secrets for future backstabbing. She had no idea that tree shadows could be used to freeze those who taunted you, the effort fleeting but lasting long enough so you could shift and tear into their skin.

The blood I ripped out using that exact trick had sunk into deep moss cushions, feeding the soil. The encircling oaks had grown taller as I chastised my enemies. Ruby red flowers had sprung up in my paws' wake.

Not the kind of magic this girl imagined. Her version was far more palatable. *One minute*, I promised, trailing behind her. One more minute, then I'd continue along my path.

After all, the man I was meeting today might be my father. Since being ejected from the Faery, it had taken me months to track down the few African American shifters of the proper age to share my DNA. More weeks had elapsed after that as I worked through the first two contenders and determine they were unrelated to me.

There was only one possibility left. One chance to find a home here in the non-fae world. It was either that or go back to my mother, who'd smiled at the sight of my bloodbath. Who, I later realized, had manipulated me into losing control.

I shook my head to dismiss the past as the girl scampered across a snowy log. She was following the tracks of a squirrel, half bent over to see them better. At the far end, she leapt to the ground then spun. "I see you!"

I froze. Seriously? I'd been outwitted by a six-year-old child?

"Yes, you, wolf! I'm talking to you!"

The girl's mittened fingers scooped up snow, patted it into a snowball. A weapon. Of course. She was frightened.

No wonder after what I'd done at the fae court. In the end, no one had died—it was hard to kill fae—but many had been forced into hibernation to heal from my rampage. And, yes, they'd used my own protective instincts to trick me into it. But I wasn't a fish. I didn't have to bite.

Instead, I was a beast. Too powerful for my own good.

But when the girl threw her projectile, she didn't use the blow to buy escape time. Instead, she watched the sphere arc up then down, landing with a plop three feet from my flared nostrils. "You're supposed to catch it," she chided, scooping up more snow for a second try.

Catch it? As in, a game? Like I'd seen young shifters play two packs ago, before I was chased out of that particular territory with my tail between my legs?

"You can do it," the girl coached. "Keep your eye on the ball. Aim for where it'll be, not where it is now."

Someone had taught this pixie physics. She watched me with such expectation.

When she tossed the second snowball, I leapt up and plucked it out of the air with my sharp teeth.

❖—————❖

Five snowballs later, I left the tutu-clad human to her own devices. She was tiring while my last possible sperm donor was waiting. So I slunk to the culvert I'd scouted out prior to sending this maybe-dad an invitation letter. Shifting in the confined space, icy metal scraped against my skin.

Ignoring the burn, I twisted to pull the pack off my back and remove the clothes I'd been wearing when I fled the world of fairy. Shirt and pants so bright they made everyone in this world stare at me. Silk slippers that had been fashionable in a realm of endless summer but here were little better than going barefoot.

Still, I didn't want to appear bestial. Remembering fae taunts, I yanked on the slippers and slithered out the culvert's far end.

Before my feet hit the ground, the man had spun to face me. Tall and broad. Darker than me by half.

He'd come alone, just like I requested. But the wolf was alert behind the older man's eyes.

My own wolf rose in answer. We bristled, human on the outside, lupine inside. If we'd been four-footed, we would have stalked in a stiff-legged circle, hunting each other's weakest points.

Neither of us attacked though. Instead, I waited and, after an endless silence, he shook his head. "I don't believe it. I used a condom. She was on the pill. And...you look exactly like her."

I looked nothing like my mother. She was full-blooded fae, with all the elegance that heritage denoted. Her skin was pale. Her scent was floral. Her fingers, when she finally pulled me away from the bloodbath, had felt like skinless bone.

"Birth control isn't 100%," I said instead of remarking upon any of that. I also didn't remark upon the fact that my mother had likely used fae magic to melt holes in the condom after lying about her own birth control. She'd wanted a half-shifter child until she realized what she was getting out of the deal.

Still wanted me, actually. But only if I was willing to come to heel and ravage on command.

"I can see that." My father took a step forward. "It's a pleasure to meet you, son. May I call you 'son'?"

I tried to nod, but my neck wasn't moving. I couldn't believe it. This really was my father. And he was accepting me so easily.

No, not so easily. He was still speaking. "But you can't stay here. Your wolf is too strong and our alpha isn't forgiving."

There it was. The cold, hard truth. Even my father didn't want the hassle of my presence.

"I understand," I told him, turning away while I battled down rage. Fur pressed up through my skin. The fae scent of persimmons rolled off me in waves.

I clenched my fists rather than succumbing to violent impulses. I wouldn't be that person a second time. Instead, I'd return to the culvert and shift then slink into the forest. I could live for a long time as a wolf in the little-traveled land at the edges of territories.

I shivered as a snowflake landed on my neck, the memory of the tutu fairy's laughter ringing in my ears. That, plus my father's voice:

"Wait."

I paused, but didn't turn. "I don't need your pity."

Only, he wasn't offering pity. His words bit deep. "Did you know that fae are a danger to our packs? That a group of us hunts them?"

"Are you threatening me, old man?" Now I did turn to face him. I'd given myself away with the scent, so I'd have to deal with the problem. Shifting here would be fast and easy. Blood would splatter across the snow like the most beautiful modern art.

My father would die, though, rather than hibernate. I closed my eyes and bit down on my tongue.

"You got that from your father," the Queen had told me when I ripped my way through obstructions rather than dancing around them. And yet...my unintentional sperm donor could easily have raised the temperature of our conversation with a growl. Instead, when I had enough self-control to open my eyes, I found that he'd bowed his head, acknowledging my wolf's superior strength.

"I'm offering you a solution," he told the ground. "You're too overbearing to join a pack, unless you want to kill their alpha. But the Samhain Shifters would take you. They'd be grateful for your assistance hunting fae."

Something dark flashed through the air between us. A phone. I'd seen these in the hands of shifters and humans alike but hadn't bothered to acquire one. After all, you needed someone to call to make the hunk of plastic worth carrying.

Still, the slim rectangle's path was predetermined. Thinking of the six-year-old, I caught it. Easy when I aimed for where the phone was going rather than where it currently was.

"Their number's programmed in," my father said. "Not mine. You need to leave. *Now.*"

My father's words pushed me away and this time he didn't stop me. Instead, his advice trailed behind as I stalked into the forest without a farewell from either of us.

"Use equal care in the human world. They're scared of black men, even if they don't know about your wolf nature…"

The sentiment behind his words shoved me past the culvert, giving me no respite to stop and shift. Instead, I let snow soak through my silk slippers, the cold outside matching the cold within.

Because I'd left Faery hoping my father would provide what my mother couldn't. But he saw the same thing in me she had.

In their eyes, I was nothing more than a beast.

Chapter 2

I did shift eventually. Considered tossing the cell phone but instead stuffed it away in my backpack with the useless fae clothing. Then I wrestled my arms through the shoulder straps and fell down onto four paws.

With nowhere in particular to go, I shouldn't have been surprised when my feet carried me back toward the tutu fairy. I didn't intend to let her see me this time. I just craved the warmth of her giggles before pushing deeper into the cold.

Instead, I heard crying. Sobs so raw she must have given up on being answered quite some time ago. I flared my nostrils. Scented blood.

Rushing out of the forest four-legged, I didn't stop to think about how I'd look to her. Yes, the girl had wanted to play with me earlier. But, earlier, I hadn't stopped to kill a rabbit and let the juices splash my chest hairs. Earlier, my eyes hadn't been full of the disillusionment of being tossed a cell phone when I asked for a helping hand.

Only, the girl didn't scream at the sight of me. Instead, she swiped one chilled hand—she'd lost her mitten—across tear-stained cheeks. "Wolf," she said as imperiously as any fae princess, "take me home."

What could I do but obey her? I didn't sidle away to shift in secrecy either. I didn't want my tutu fairy to think, even for a second, that I was abandoning her to the cold.

Plus, would she trust my human side as easily as she did my lupine form? I couldn't risk it. Instead, I broke one of the few rules werewolves seemed to abide by. I shimmered upward right there in front of her, using my backpack to cover my privates. I spoke the moment my human vocal cords allowed.

"Don't be afraid. I promise I won't hurt you."

"Of course you won't, wolf." Six-year-olds believed in magic. She didn't bat an eyelash at my transformation. Instead, she pointed in the direction where suburbia impinged on the forest. I could make out a house just far enough away so her screams hadn't been heeded. "I live over there."

Destination was sorted, but I needed to look more human for the next part. So rather than plucking her up immediately, I asked, "What happened, little fairy?" as I pulled on flowing trousers.

Well, the clothes had been flowing months ago. Now they were ripped and stained. The bells at the ankles, though, still jingled. The girl reached out to tap one. "They're pretty."

It was the closest thing to a compliment I'd ever received, so I batted it back at her. "You're prettier."

The girl, I noted, hadn't answered my question, but I could put two and two together. The pine behind her had limbs arranged like stair steps. But where snow had been knocked off the lowest branches, the bark was icy smooth.

"You tried to climb and fell."

"The tree dropped me," she corrected. "My leg hurts. My hand too."

Rather than pulling on my shirt, I draped it around her shoulders. The silk wasn't much of a barrier against the cold, but it was all I had. "I'm going to pick you up. That might hurt even worse," I warned.

She closed her eyes and pinched her nose with her mittened hand as if she was about to be dunked under water. Her voice was nasal as she said. "Do it. I'm tough."

I did. And she was.

⁂

Her house was stone, something I'd never seen in Faery. The door, when I reached out to tap it, burnt my hand.

Still, I didn't jerk back. A fleeting touch of steel wouldn't kill me. And my tutu fairy was shivering in my arms.

She'd been in the snow too long. Even I could tell that and I'd never spent time around humans. Her mittenless hand, despite being stuck in my armpit to warm it, remained red and frigid. There was ice lining her hair.

No wonder the man who opened the door looked like he wanted to pound me into hamburger. It didn't help that my fairy turned into a ball of wriggle when she saw him. "Daddy!" she cried, leaping out of my arms.

His brows lowered in confusion as he caught her. "I thought you were in your room."

She whispered her answer into his shoulder. "I climbed out the window."

Their exchange gave me the space to back up. One step. Two steps. "She fell out of a tree," I told the father. "Don't touch her leg."

My warning came too late. The girl twisted, her father grabbed hold of her knee to steady her...then my tutu fairy screamed, the shriek high enough to shatter glass.

Then a woman was there behind them. She took in the scene with one furious glance. Unlike the tutu fairy's father, she didn't flinch back from the sight of me. Instead, it was as if I didn't even exist.

"I'm starting the car," she told her mate. There were coats in her hand so fast she might as well have possessed fae magic. One draped over the child, one over her husband, one over herself.

Keys jangled. The door slammed shut, closing all of us out into the snow together. Then the two adults with the tutu fairy in the father's arms were rushing down the steps toward their vehicle. They piled in, mother in the driver's seat, father in the passenger seat, six-year-old in his lap.

The car roared to life then screeched to a stop as it hit the end of the driveway. The woman's window slid down.

"You," the mother pointed at me. "Come tomorrow for dinner."

The tutu fairy waved goodbye with her mittened hand as they sped off.

Chapter 3

I shifted back to fur form at the edge of the forest. Drank from the stream. Found a dry cavity pressed up against an upturned root mass and curled into a ball to sleep.

In the morning, the snow sparkled like jewels. As beautiful as the land of Faery. More beautiful, actually, because I was alone.

No shifters to chase me out of their territory. No fae to bend me to their will. For a while, it was paradise.

Aloneness palled by the time the sun hit its zenith. I needed to make a decision. Return to the Unseelie Court where my mother would welcome me...and use me? Kill an alpha and take his place within a werewolf pack? Try to blend into the masses of humanity, despite endless expanses of metal and a skin color that made strangers flinch?

Being alone wasn't so bad, I tried to tell myself. I could head north, up to the Arctic Circle where wolves were commonplace. I could fall so deep into fur form that I might never come back out again.

And yet, as the sun dipped above snow turned soft and slushy, I was still in the same fragment of forest I'd woken up in. In the interim, I'd sniffed the pine tree and found the barest hint of fae magic. The child's gibberish incantation must have given someone a toehold on this world that they'd used to wreak mischief. I had to make sure she was alright.

I didn't know the timing of human dinner, but sunset seemed appropriate. Shifting to humanity at the edge of suburbia, I donned the same silk slippers and pants.

When I knocked this time, I used my backpack to shield my hand from the metal. This time, the tutu fairy's mother was the one who opened the door.

"Did he come?" The six-year-old's voice rang through the house.

"He came," the mother answered, her whole voice smiling. Turning to me, though, her brows lowered. "I'd offer to take your coat, but you don't even have a shirt." She reached out and pulled something soft off a hook beside her. "Put this on. You're making me cold."

I shook my head. "I'm not staying."

But the mother didn't withdraw the clothing, so I yanked the thick warmth over my head. When I was able to see again, my tutu fairy was there between us. Same crazy skirt, this time layered over tights striped in every hue of the rainbow. Her exuberance was unquenched but crutches slowing her forward flight by approximately fifty percent.

"The doctor gave me a dog bandaid," she said, showing off a colorful sticker on her wrist where she didn't need one. "I asked for a *wolf*. Like you."

I leaned in as if looking at the bandage, but really I was smelling her. Nothing but child. The fae had worked their mischief and left. I could go as well now.

This time, it was the mother's gesture that froze me. She ran a hand through her daughter's hair, reassurance for both of them. Then she remarked upon the tutu fairy's wolf comment. "She's very imaginative."

The tutu fairy wilted at her mother's disbelief. I couldn't let that stand.

"Imagination powers the world," I murmured. The tutu fairy smiled like the reemergence of the sun.

So that was solved also. Still, I lingered at the border between cold and warmth. I knew which direction I needed to travel toward, but I couldn't get my feet moving out the door.

The tutu fairy had her own ideas. "Wait until you see what we're eating!"

Her tiny hand dragged me forward. It was an awkward maneuver with her crutches, but she managed. Unable to resist, I took two steps deeper inside.

Then the father was filling the open archway between entry hall and dining room, breaking my connection to the tutu fairy. "I hope you like pot roast." Despite the implied invitation, he pressed into my personal space. He wasn't so sure he wanted me there.

I wasn't so sure I wanted to be there either. I inched backwards, hand reaching for the doorknob, anticipating the burn.

Before I could push myself to accept the pain, the tutu fairy poked her head back around the corner. "The carrots and meat and gravy are good," she informed me. "But you'll hate the peas."

Meat? I faced fully forward again, my eyebrows lifting. In Faery, no one ate meat. The act was considered uncivilized. Bestial.

I did though. I consumed raw rabbits and day-old roadkill with relish.

And now, it appeared, I ate pot roast.

Somehow, I found myself at a table. Not a fancy banquet table, but a cozy wooden oval with plastic place mats. The rectangles were decorated with rainbows and unicorns.

"You're supposed to put your napkin in your lap," the tutu fairy informed me. "It's civilized."

"Honey," her mother chided.

I shook out the paper napkin the same way she had and slid it over my silken trousers. "Thank you for the instructions."

"Good." Nodding her praise, the tutu fairy clutched her fork as if it was a dagger. No one corrected her cutlery skills.

Instead, we ate together, the meal more earthy than anything I'd consumed in Faery but also more delicious. Or maybe the savory sensation lingering on my tongue came from the laughter around the table. The way my tutu fairy spilled the peas off her plate accidentally on purpose.

"Oops," she said, eyes and mouth both curving sideways.

"I know you hate them," her father observed. "But peas will heal you up fast so you can get off those crutches."

"Okay." The tutu fairy ate two green spheres. "Is that enough?"

No one forced her to pop more into her mouth.

Later, her father led me into a back room alone. Now it would come. The hamburger pounding.

Or rather, the *attempted* hamburger pounding. My wolf would spill out at the first hint of danger. The memory of blood mingled with pot roast on my tongue.

We can't, I told my wolf.

We have to survive, my wolf rebutted.

Unaware of our silent conversation, the man dug into drawers and pulled out clothes much heftier than silk. "They don't fit me any-more." He patted his belly. "Too much pot roast."

There was no such thing as too much pot roast. Cooked meat was nothing like raw meat. The seasoning had tasted like love.

So I accepted this gift also. Dropped my silken garments onto the carpet and shook out the human clothing. My ass was bare when the tutu fairy invaded, my backpack under her armpit.

"I put in our number," she told me, steadying her crutches so she could withdraw the phone and hold it out to me. "You need more numbers."

I yanked up the pants fast despite the fact her father had stepped between us to preserve my modesty and her innocence. The metal snap burned my fingers but I managed to close it. Only then did I reach for my phone.

"Thanks," I told the tutu fairy. Then, turning to her father. "Thanks for everything. But I've got to go."

"Are you sure?" This was the mother. She appeared to be tethered to her child by an invisible connection, one I envied. "It's dark outside. The couch pulls out into a bed."

"I'm fine. Really."

Better than fine with this memory of family to guide me. Outside, I stood for one long moment in the street, watching joy pour out through uncurtained windows. The tutu fairy was draping a string of lights in a crooked zigzag across a cut evergreen. She'd fallen from a pine tree yesterday, but today she was gracing another with her exuberant love.

And fae had tried to kill her. For no particular reason. Just because she was there in front of them.

Fae didn't belong on this earth, but I wasn't going back to my mother. And, anyway, I was only half fae.

So I pulled out the cell phone and dialed a number. Not the tutu fairy's. I'd save that one as a reminder.

Instead, I yanked on the thread my father had offered. As soon as the line connected, I opened with: "I was told you hunt fae."

Chapter 4

I gave the shifter who answered my true name as collateral. A way to ensure I wasn't like my mother. That whichever wolf I worked with could overpower me if I went rogue.

In exchange, she promised we'd only send fae back to Faery rather than killing them. She taught me to keep my wolf quiet when necessary. Gave me words that let me walk through wolf territories without hiding my existence or baring my teeth.

That was ten years ago. Ten times since then, I've called the tutu fairy's number and dropped by for a meal of pot roast. Those meals remind me why I chose this world instead of the beauty of the fae homeland. They remind me that saving lives is worth living for.

Like my tutu fairy taught, I don't look at where I am now but instead at where I'm going. Which is why I knew the moment I saw my mate that she was my future. An alpha, hard and tough as my handler but with forgotten glitter gracing her cheekbones. The silver sparkled like snowflakes when her friend dumped hot chocolate over her head to get rid of me. She glowered at me from beneath dripping hair with the force of an enraged werewolf.

I didn't leave though. How could I when I finally saw where my snowball was flying?

But that's a story from another year and for another wolf to tell.

❖ ııı————ıoı————ıı ❖

I hope you enjoyed this glimpse into Rune's life. You can read that other story told by the alpha with glitter on her cheekbones in <u>Charmed Wolf</u>.

Ambush

Spoiler alert:

Minor spoilers for the <u>Moon Marked Trilogy</u>. Probably safe to read, though, unless you're a real stickler.

✦ ⊩————ıⅢ————⊩ ✦

An ambush. Wolf hairs pushed through human skin. Teeth sharpened.

But I clenched my fists until wolf features receded. And I kept my voice calm as I asked, "What exactly are you suggesting?"

My alpha had broached the topic originally. But it was his teenage sister-in-law, Kira, who attacked next. "You could try walking with a book on your head, Tank. It would force you to keep your chin up."

Suiting actions to words, she plunked a heavy textbook down on my noggin while snatching away the phone I'd been pretending to be engrossed in. All while prancing atop the three-foot-high wall that kept her eyes sixteen inches above mine.

The kid was a fox with the instincts of a wolf. Higher ground. An effective strategy to counteract her smaller size.

I was amused, so I obeyed her. Swallowed down bile and kept my chin up, despite the passing humans who took one look at me and quickly found something far more interesting to peer at on the other side of the street.

"You know, when I first met you, I just thought you were phone obsessed," Mai observed. This was my alpha's mate. Kira's sister. A key component of the ambush. "I didn't realize you were *traumatized*."

"I'm not traumatized." Even to my own ears, the gritty words didn't sound believable. I wasn't *traumatized*, though. I was doing my best not to scar passersby.

Case in point: an ancient woman prying herself out of the passenger-side seat of a station wagon took one look at me and lost her grip on the door frame. She would have hit the ground if Gunner—my alpha—hadn't swooped in to break her fall.

"Oh my." If the woman had been a couple of decades younger, the transition from terror to swoon might have been something other than amusing. As it was, Mai had to disentangle her mate before the human could get handsy.

"It was nice meeting you," Mai said, bestowing the human with a smile that seemed to glow from the inside.

"Aren't you sweet?" the woman replied, patting Mai on the cheek.

That was the normal human reaction to jovial werewolves and fox shifters. Something about our contentment attracted them. As if we were loyal hounds snoozing on the hearth or puppies clambering out of a cardboard box too small to hold all of us.

I didn't give off that vibe. And not because I wasn't content. Current ambush aside, I was happier than I'd ever been. Over the past few years, Gunner had molded his pack into a seamless family. I was busy doctoring and lawyering, my favorite way to keep hands and mind busy. And Kira and I had moved on from learning magic tricks to juggling in our spare time.

"Maybe not on the wall," I suggested as my phone was swept up into the air along with an apple from Kira's backpack and a rock gathered from beneath the girl's feet.

"Keep your chin level," Kira countered, "or you'll scratch my book when it hits the ground."

"Better not scratch the book," I muttered. But my mouth quirked up into a smile.

I'd never had a little sister, which perhaps explained the enjoyment I got out of Kira's sass. Either that, or the fact that she wasn't scared of my features. It must have been something about fox shifters, because neither Kira nor Mai twitched when my lips curved up.

Of course, smiling was a bad idea. I knew that. Tried not to do it except around these three, the core components of my adopted family.

Because a cat on a porch took one look at me and puffed up to the size of a basketball. It screeched out terror and fled into the darkness under the porch supports.

The smile slide off my face.

"Stop that." Mai's fingers slid around my elbow, forcing me to bend the arm and accommodate her. "If you want to smile, *smile*."

"Which returns me to my point," Gunner growled. Unlike the females, he was pure wolf. Intent upon the hunt, willing to stalk his prey until it made one wrong move and gave him a clear shot at its jugular.

In case you were wondering, I was the prey. Or, rather, my dating life was.

"No unattached females in our clan can see past my face," I explained for the ten thousandth time. "If I'd known outpack territories were going to dry up so quickly, I would have gone lone wolf years ago. Not that there were many unaffiliated females running around even then. But that's water over the dam. I'm content as I am. I'm…"

"Ack!"

Kira's shriek was all the warning I needed. We'd practiced this move dozens of times. She tumbled, I caught her juggling objects, spun her 360 degrees, then set her on her feet without getting in the way of the aerial objects' figure-eight path.

We'd always performed our routine over padded floor mats, however. Not over asphalt. Still, I caught and released my cell phone and the apple, sending both soaring as my hands closed around Kira's waist.

My head stayed steady. Had to if it didn't want to dislodge her precious math book.

"Whee!" *Kira's* smile didn't scare nearby humans as she nudged the rock upward and enjoyed being twirled. A toddler laughed and pointed. A dog busted out a joyful bark.

Her shoes struck the pavement just as my cell phone thudded into her waiting fingers. My gaze slid sideway to gauge Gunner's response.

Because this was the first time he'd seen Kira's newest trick, and I hadn't been looking forward to the moment. Kira might act like a kid still, but at seventeen she'd developed curves that made me wince and made certain pack mates perk up and take notice.

I did my best to shield her from inappropriate male attention, just like Gunner did. But it would be understandable if Kira's over-protective brother-in-law didn't give me the benefit of the doubt.

"You could just wait ten years until it's not creepy and marry me," Kira observed, eyes still on her juggling.

I winced. Yeah, that was exactly the way to prevent Gunner from going batshit on me for the crime of touching his kid sister's waist.

Not.

"Still creepy," I observed. And while I should have rounded my shoulders and prepared to accept my alpha's displeasure...I didn't. I couldn't. That was why I'd ended up with the scare-elderly-ladies face.

Instead, the wolf behind my eyes bored into Gunner. I couldn't shift here, but I could subvocalize a growl. A warning that his wolf wasn't much tougher than mine.

Predictably, Gunner's hand lashed out...but he wasn't punching me. Instead, he snatched the book off my head then clasped my shoulder. "Relax. I trust you. Which is why I'm asking you to do this for me. Two weeks with werewolves from other packs. Keep your chin up. Smile occasionally. Try not to rip anybody's throat out."

"Yes, we can manage without you," Mai interrupted before I could ask the obvious question. "You're essential, but even essential wolves are allowed vacations."

"And," Kira added, changing over to the ultra-complicated Mill's Mess juggling pattern while landing the final blow in the ambush her alpha had set up, "don't come home without a mate."

Want to see what happens when Tank follows his alpha's advice? Pick up a copy of <u>Moon Glamour</u> *for a standalone adventure full of temporary pack, sweet romance, and fae.*

Inappropriate

The asshole was pointing a gun at my mate. No wonder my hand clamped down around his wrist as my wolf nearly leapt out of my human skin. "Halt," I growled, squeezing hard enough to grind bone against bone.

And Skye laughed at me while prying my fingers loose. "Ryder." One, two. "I'm good. Really." Three, four. "We agreed on this. Remember?"

Her touch was profoundly soothing. By the time she reached my thumb, I was ready to listen. Still, I settled my best glare on the gun wielder as I warned: "Don't hurt her or you'll regret it."

"Tattoos hurt," the artist replied, uninterested in my dominance display. He was human, after all, and unaffected by lupine warnings.

He'd be more interested when I found him in a dark alley and ripped his throat out...

"Ryder," Skye warned a second time. "I'm aware that tattoos are painful. It will be worth it."

The tattoo gun slid closer to her bare ankle. I growled a second time. The artist set down the gun and cracked his neck. "Look, if you're not ready, I get it. Take some time. Think it over. We have a few openings next week..."

Skye's teeth sharpened ever so slightly, her eyes the ones flashing wolf this time. "We're doing this. Today. Both of us. Right, Ryder?"

And...my wolf settled. I loved it when our mate decided on something and turned ferocious.

If only her ferocity today didn't mean she was about to be stabbed hundreds of times...

"Ryder?" she repeated.

I shook myself, accepting the inevitable. Still... I cleared my throat. "Ink me first."

"Whatever." The human shrugged then got down to business. I had very little art on the lower half of my body, so it was easy to fit in one short word wrapped around my ankle. I was prepared for the minor pains then surprised when I didn't feel a thing.

"You're..." I started, glaring at Skye before moving our conversation to our mate bond. *"You're taking away the pain."*

"I can handle it." Her silent voice was amused. *"You've forgotten this isn't my first tattoo."*

It was her first intentional one, though. Her first one created for the sake of art and bonding rather than with the fae intention of stealing energy she didn't want to part with.

I only realized I was growling again when the tattoo gun lifted off my flesh. "Need a break?"

Skye and I spoke in perfect unison. "No."

And, half an hour later when it was time to ink the same word onto her ankle, I decided turnabout was fair play. Grabbing our mate bond in one fist, I teased it across her skin like a feather duster. Cheek. Neck. Lower...

Skye wriggled, nearly purring from pleasure. The tattoo artist muttered something a human wouldn't have heard under his breath, so I ignored language that wasn't suitable for Skye's delicate ears.

"See, didn't even hurt," Skye told me when both of our tattoos were finished. She was right. Nothing hurt the way I thought it would when we were together.

We stretched out our ankles until they were side by side, hers elegant, mine fat and hairy. "Care to share the significance?" asked the tattoo artist as he prepped our bandages.

Skye laughed, the sound so beautiful she could almost have been fae. "Just an inside joke," she told him. "Something we share. Something that brought us together."

I smiled at the identical words, upside-down but easily readable. *Inappropriate.* Our bond was anything but.